Shifty McGifty
AND
SLIPPERY SAM

THE
MISSING
MASTERPIECE

Spot me on every page!

First published 2018 by Nosy Crow Ltd
The Crow's Nest, 14 Baden Place, Crosby Row, London SE1 1YW
www.nosycrow.com

ISBN 978 0 85763 974 5 (HB)
ISBN 978 0 85763 975 2 (PB)

Nosy Crow and associated logos are trademarks and/or registered trademarks
of Nosy Crow Ltd.

Text © Tracey Corderoy 2018
Illustrations © Steven Lenton 2018

A CIP catalogue record for this book is available from the British Library.

Papers used by Nosy Crow are made from wood grown in sustainable forests.

Printed in Turkey
10 9 8 7 6 5 4 3 2 1 (HB)
10 9 8 7 6 5 4 3 2 1 (PB)

For Mark, Anna
and Charlotte.
Such happy
memories of Paris!
T.C. xx

For Emma
'Book Sniffer'
O'Donovan for
being a pawfect pal!
S.L.

Shifty McGifty
AND
SLIPPERY SAM
THE MISSING MASTERPIECE

Tracey Corderoy

Illustrated by
Steven Lenton

ADVENTURE

HOME

nosy crow

When **you** were a baby and still in your pram,
there lived two daft **robbers** called Shifty and Sam.
They tried to be sneaky, but never quite could.
So now they are **bakers** who try to be good!

They once baked in . . .

. . . Paris! So – ooh la la – smart,
with cafés and cheese shops
and fine works of art.

"And here's where we're baking.
Look, Sam!" Shifty cried.
"It's Galerie Bonbon!
Quick, let's go inside."

Then Sam saw a poster. He read it. "Oh my!
There's a fox who steals paintings,
called Cunningham Sly!"

"Come on," Shifty nodded, "we've no time to worry.
We can't hang about, Sam. We really must hurry.
The art exhibition will start in an hour.
We've **still** got to bake a huge gingerbread tower!"

"Oh yes!" Sam remembered. "The Mayor's coming too.
You're right – let's get baking. We've so much to do!"

NOUVELLE
EXPOSITION
'Classique'
OUVRE
ce soir!

The way to the kitchen was through a big hall,
where beautiful paintings adorned every wall.

"*Psst!* See those red curtains?"
Sam pointed a paw.
"They're hiding a masterpiece,
Shifty – I'm sure!"

Pug with a
Pearl Earring

Son of
Man's
Best Friend

Frida Collie

But Shifty was heading back out to the van
because they'd forgotten their best copper pan.

Sam soon found the kitchen, where to his surprise,
he stumbled upon a smart fox with bright eyes.
"Au revoir!" called the fox, heading through the back door.
But Sam had the feeling he'd seen him before.

"Do I know you?" asked Sam.
But the fox shook his head.
"Monsieur, I'm afraid you're mistaken!" he said.
"You see, I'm an **artist** and paint all day long.
Which means that I rarely go out,
so . . . you're wrong."

The fox tapped his painting, all carefully wrapped.
"Is that *yours*? Wow, I've met a real artist!" Sam clapped.

Sam raced to tell Shifty, now back in the hall,
but stopped right in front of the masterpiece wall.

The curtains were open, the wall was quite . . .

bare!

"I peeped," Shifty gulped.
"But the painting's . . . not there!"

"Remember that poster of Cunningham Sly,
that sneaky fox-robber?" Sam said with a cry.
"I saw him just now with a parcel I'm SURE!
I think he was sneaking it out of the door!

He must have just stolen the painting! Oh no!"
"Don't worry – we'll catch him!" cried Shifty. "Let's go!"

Outside in the city, they drove like the wind.
"That cunning old fox won't escape us!" Sam grinned.
Beep beep!
Shifty tooted and Sam gripped his seat,
as buns, tarts and croissants bounced off down the street!

Then close to the river Sam let out a shout,
"That's him! That's the fox that I saw sneaking out!"
They raced to the water but only to spy . . .

. . . a getaway dinghy belonging to Sly!

The thief hopped on board with the painting held tight,
and called to the boys with a smirk of delight . . .

"I'm Cunningham Sly
and you'll never catch me.
For I am as cunning
as cunning can be!"

The fox sped away.

"He's escaping!" Sam cried.

"He hasn't won yet!" Shifty quickly replied.

He flicked up a switch on the dashboard and . . .

...boom! –
their van was a speedboat.
And off they went –

ZOOOOOOM!

The chase was back on, but the robber was fast.
"We're catching him now!" Shifty shouted at last.
He revved up the engine. Then with a huge crash
a wave hit Sly's dinghy and, suddenly . . .

...SPLASH!

"Oh help! I can't swim!"
called the fox with a shout.
Sam tossed him a lifebuoy
to help fish him out.

They rescued the painting
as Sly coughed and spluttered.
"You've ruined my BEST robbing waistcoat!"
he muttered.

At Galerie Bonbon, they opened the door,
and marched the wet robber across the clean floor.
Some policemen were waiting to take Sly away.
They thanked Sam and Shifty for saving the day.

Then Sam held the masterpiece out. "Here you go!"
He tore off the wrapping, but then cried . . .

"Oh no!"

The painting was splattered
in greenish-grey grime,
and bits from the river,
and watery slime.

"But, boys!" the Mayor chuckled, his cheeks rosy-red.
"The painting Sly stole is a **fake** one!" he said.
"We thought he would strike so we swapped them around.
And here is the **real** masterpiece – safe and sound!"

Bone-a-Lisa

"But **YOU** caught the thief – so well done!"
cried the Mayor.
"Bravo!" cheered the crowd
with their hats in the air.

At eight it was time for the party to start.

So Shifty and Sam brought in their work of art . . . .

"Oh, boys!" beamed the Mayor, and he patted his tummy.

"That gingerbread tower looks so –
ooh la la – yummy!"

Next day Paris buzzed
with the talk of a team
who captured sly robbers
AND baked like a dream!

Sam opened the paper.
"Look, Shifty!" he cried . . .

... "Now that's a **real** masterpiece!"
Shifty replied.